NEW BELIEVER'S SERIES

WATCHMAN NEE

WITHSTANDING THE DEVIL

21

Living Stream Ministry
Anaheim, CA • www.lsm.org

First Edition, November 1997.

ISBN 978-1-57593-977-3

Published by

Living Stream Ministry
2431 W. La Palma Ave., Anaheim, CA 92801 U.S.A.
P. O. Box 2121, Anaheim, CA 92814 U.S.A.

Printed in the United States of America

13 14 15 16 17 18 / 11 10 9 8 7 6 5

WITHSTANDING THE DEVIL

Scripture Reading: James 4:7; 1 Pet. 5:8-9; 2 Cor. 2:11

The devil is known also as Satan (Rev. 12:9). He was first a cherubim, created by God (Ezek. 28:12-14), and he was an archangel (Rev. 12:7; Matt. 25:41). Later, he rebelled against God by uplifting himself to be equal to God. Because of this, God judged him (Isa. 14:12-15; Ezek. 28:15-19) and he became Satan, the adversary of God. In the original text the word *Satan* means "an opposer, an adversary." The devil opposes everything that God does. In addition, he always sets himself against God's children.

We want to look at the way the devil attacks God's children and how they withstand him.

I. SATAN'S WORK

We will look at Satan's work in four aspects.

A. Satan's Work in the Human Mind

Second Corinthians 10:4-5 says, "For the weapons of our warfare are not fleshly but powerful before God for the overthrowing of strongholds, as we overthrow reasonings and every high thing rising up against the knowledge of God, and take captive every thought unto the obedience of Christ." This shows us that Satan uses every high thing as a stronghold to surround man's thought. In order for the Lord to gain us, He must first overthrow the strongholds of Satan. He must do this before He can charge into man's thought and take it captive.

1. Satan's Reasonings and Temptations

What are reasonings? This word in Greek can be translated "imagination" or "thought." Satan often surrounds us with many imaginations. Men are foolish; they think that these thoughts are their own. Actually, they are the strong-holds of Satan, and they prevent the mind from submitting to Christ. Often Satan injects a kind of imagination into our mind. If we think this imagination is from ourselves, we fall into his snare. Often thoughts develop which have no basis in fact; they are merely imaginations. Many so-called sins are imaginary in nature; they are not real. Many of the so-called problems among the brothers and sisters come from our imagination; they have no factual basis. Often Satan injects a wild thought into our mind, and we are completely oblivious to his work. When he injects a sudden thought into our mind and we accept it, we are accepting his work. If we reject this thought, we reject his work. Many thoughts are not our own; they are actually concocted by Satan. We must learn to reject these thoughts from Satan.

Most of Satan's temptations come through the mind. Satan realizes that God's children will rise up and withstand him vehemently if he attacks openly. This is the reason he tempts us by sneaking in stealthily and planting a thought in our mind unconsciously. Once the thought gets into us, we begin to think about it. If the more we dwell on a thought the more we feel justified and right, we have fallen into his snare. The thought that we have accepted is Satan's temptation. If we reject Satan's attacks in our mind, we will shut off the most vulnerable entrance of his temptations.

Many problems among God's children are problems in the mind; they are not real problems. Sometimes when you see a brother or a sister, you may feel that he or she has a problem with you or that there is a distance between you. This may result in a barrier between you. Actually, there is nothing between you. The so-called problem is merely Satan's attack in your mind or the mind of your brother or sister. Such prob-lems are unnecessary problems. God's children must reject sudden thoughts and sudden feelings. They must learn never to give in to Satan.

Here, we need to issue a warning. We should not be overly concerned about thoughts from Satan. There are people who go to one extreme of paying no attention at all to Satan's thoughts. There are also people who go to the other extreme of paying too much attention to thoughts from Satan. A person can easily be cheated if he is not alert to thoughts from Satan. At the same time, a person can lose his mental sanity if he is obsessed about thoughts from Satan. If a person pays too much attention to Satan's temptations, his mind will become confused, and he will easily become a prey to Satan's snares. As soon as a person's eyes are not focused on the Lord, he will find himself in trouble. On the one hand, we need to see that Satan does attack our mind. On the other hand, we need to realize that as soon as we reject his attacks, that is the end of them. If a person has to reject Satan day and night, something is wrong with his mind; he is heading down the wrong road. On the one hand, we must be familiar with his wiles; if we are ignorant of them we will be cheated. On the other hand, we cannot be overly concerned because that will also lead us into deception. As soon as our eyes are set on him, he has gained what he wants. This distraction will render us useless, and we will become obsessed with his thoughts day and night. Any brother or sister who is overly concerned with such thoughts has already been deceived. We must learn to maintain a proper balance. An excessive concern is wrong. If a person's mind is constantly worried about thoughts from Satan, he is in reality giving ground to Satan to enter into him. We must never go to the extreme.

2. How to Reject Thoughts from Satan

How do we reject thoughts from Satan? It is easy to reject these thoughts. God has given us our mind; it is ours, not Satan's. We are the only ones who have the right to use our mind; Satan has no authority over our mind. All we need to do is not allow him to think. Satan can only usurp our mind with deception. He will give us a thought, and we may think that this thought is ours. Actually, it is from Satan. As soon as we recognize that it is not ours, we have overcome.

Satan always tempts and attacks a person by stealthy, surreptitious, and covert ways. He does not shout loudly, "Here I come!" Instead, he deceives with lies and falsehood. He does not let us know that he is the one who is doing the work. Once we are aware of an attack from Satan and expose him and his disguise, it will be easy to withstand him. The Lord Jesus said, "You shall know the truth, and the truth shall set you free" (John 8:32). The truth is the fact. We will be set free once we know the fact. The power of Satan is in his lies; once his lies fail, his power is gone. Therefore, as soon as we realize that Satan is attacking us and that this is the fact, we are freed. Some children of God say with their mouth that Satan is the instigator behind everything, but their spirit has no assurance that those things are actually from Satan. Although they say that they are withstanding Satan, they do not know the reality of Satan's work. As a result, they cannot withstand him. However, as soon as they identify Satan's work, they can withstand him, and as soon as they withstand him, he flees.

Satan attacks our mind mainly through deception. He makes us think that his thoughts are ours when in reality they are from him. Once we expose his lies, we will reject the thought from him. To withstand means to refuse. When Satan gives us a thought, we should say, "I do not want it." This is what it means to withstand. When he injects one thought into us, we should say, "I do not take this." When he injects another thought into us, we should repeat, "I do not accept this." If we do this, he will not be able to do anything with us. One servant of God in the Middle Ages said, "You cannot stop birds from flying over your head, but you can at least stop them from nesting in your hair." This is a good word. We cannot stop Satan from tempting us. However, we can stop him from nesting, from gaining a beachhead in us. This power is ours. If we ignore the thoughts that enter our mind, these thoughts will stop.

On the positive side, we need to exercise our mind. Many people have lazy minds. This makes it easy for Satan's thoughts to lodge in them. Philippians 4:8 says, "What things are true, what things are dignified, what things are righteous, what things are pure, what things are lovely, what things are well spoken of, if there is any virtue and if any praise, take account of these things." We can take account of spiritual matters. We need to exercise our mind concerning spiritual matters. If a person always sets his mind on sinful things, Satan can easily inject his thoughts into him, because his thoughts and Satan's thoughts are not much different. But if we always set our mind on spiritual things, Satan will not be able to inject his thoughts into us easily. Satan is able to inject his thoughts into many people because they are passive, because they have too much spare time, or because their thoughts are unclean in the first place. There is another point that deserves attention: Our mind must not be attracted to satanic thoughts. There are many people whose minds are attracted to satanic thoughts. They have no interest in the wonderful, spiritual experiences of other brothers. Yet they become very interested when it comes to gossip. Since they love Satan's work, they cannot reject satanic thoughts. We need to hate Satan's work in order to reject his thoughts. All filthy thoughts that damage one's fellowship with the Lord and love for the Lord are from Satan. These thoughts will not come to us if we are not attracted to them in the first place. But if we incline our heart toward these things, they will come to us easily. Therefore, we must learn to reject everything that comes from Satan.

We must pay special attention to rejecting all filthy thoughts. Satan always places filthy thoughts in man to induce man to sin. The starting point is one filthy thought. If we allow it to continue, it will bear the fruit of sin. Therefore, we must refuse any thought that comes from Satan.

However, there is a great problem: What should we do if the thought refuses to leave after we have rejected it? We need to realize that we only need to withstand unwanted thoughts once. Withstanding is a one-time act; we should never withstand twice. James 4:7 says, "Withstand the devil, and he will flee from you." This verse says to withstand the devil and the devil will flee. We must believe that when we withstand the devil, he will flee. It is wrong to continue withstanding for fear that the devil is still around. Whose words do we believe? The Bible says, "Withstand...he will flee." If there is a voice within that suggests that he has not fled, whose voice is it? It is Satan's voice! Many people choose to believe Satan's words. Therefore, they lose. We must declare after we have withstood him, "I have already withstood the devil. He is gone from me."

The feeling that he is still lurking around is a lie; it is not real, and it is not from the Lord. He must run. He has no ground to stay. We must be clear that it is right to withstand once, but wrong to withstand a second time. The first withstanding glorifies God's name. The second withstanding questions God's Word.

Many people make the mistake of checking with their feelings after they have withstood the devil. They ask, "Is the devil gone?" Their feeling tells them that he is not gone, and they try to withstand him again. Once there is a second withstanding, be sure there will be a third, a fourth, even a hundredth, and a thousandth. In the end we will feel as if we are completely helpless in rejecting it. But if we ignore him completely after we have withstood his temptation once, we will experience victory. We must care for the fact of God's Word and ignore our own feelings. The fact is that as soon as we withstand the devil, he flees. If we think that he has not fled after we have withstood him, we are being deceived by our feeling. If we believe this feeling, the devil will come back. We must learn to believe God's glorious words. Once we have withstood him once, there is no need to withstand him a second time because the matter has been settled already.

These are the issues relating to Satan's work in man's mind. We must realize that Satan attacks man's mind. We should reject any thought from Satan. At the same time, we should realize that once we reject his thoughts, the matter is finished. Furthermore, we must not be overly concerned with his attacks. Otherwise, our mind will be thrown into confusion, and we will be ensnared by the devil.

B. Satan's Work on Man's Body

The Bible shows us clearly that many physical diseases are the result of Satan's attack.

The fever of Peter's mother-in-law was an attack from Satan, and the Lord Jesus rebuked the fever (Luke 4:39). Something must have a personality before the Lord can rebuke it. We cannot rebuke a cup or a chair; we can only rebuke something that has a personality. Fever is a symptom; the Lord could not rebuke the symptom. But Satan was behind the symptom with a personality of his own. Therefore, as soon as the Lord rebuked the fever, it was gone. In Mark 9 we see a dumb and deaf child. In man's eyes dumbness and deafness are sicknesses. But the Lord Jesus rebuked the unclean spirit, saying, "Dumb and deaf spirit, I order you, come out of him and enter into him no more" (v. 25). The dumbness and deafness of the child were outward symptoms of his demon possession; they were not ordinary illnesses. We must realize that many sicknesses are medically defined diseases. But there are many sicknesses that are actually attacks from the devil. The Bible does not say that the Lord healed the sickness but that He rebuked it. The boils on Job's body could not be healed by medicine; they were not medical illnesses; they were attacks from the devil. Unless one first deals with the devil, he has no way to deal with such sicknesses.

We admit that illnesses often occur through man's negligence of natural laws. However, it can quite often be the result of Satan's attack. In such a case one only has to ask the Lord to rebuke the sickness, and it will go away. This type of sickness often comes and goes away suddenly. It is an attack from Satan rather than an ordinary illness.

The complication lies in the fact that Satan does not want us to uncover and expose the illnesses he has inflicted. He always hides behind natural symptoms and makes us think that every sickness is the result of natural causes. If we allow him to hide behind these natural symptoms, our illness will not go away. Once we expose his work and rebuke him, the sickness will go away. One Christian had a very high fever and suffered greatly. He could not sleep and did not understand what was happening to him. Later, he was convinced that it was Satan's work. He prayed to the Lord about it, and the next day the fever went away.

When a Christian becomes sick, he should first find the cause for his illness. He should ask: Is there any proper reason for this sickness? Is this out of natural causes or is it an attack from Satan? If there is not a proper reason for the illness and you discover that it is indeed an attack from Satan, you should withstand him and reject him.

The work of Satan on man's body results not only in illness but also in death. Satan was a murderer from the beginning, in the same way that he was a liar from the beginning (John 8:44). We should withstand not only Satan's sickness but also his murdering. All thought of death is from Satan. Every notion of death as a means to escape from anything is from Satan. Satan made Job think of death. He did this not only to Job but also to every child of God. All notions of suicide, death wishes, and premature death are temptations from Satan. He tempts man to sin, and he also tempts man to die. Even thoughts of danger during one's travels are Satan's attacks. We must reject these thoughts whenever they come and not allow them to remain in us.

C. Satan's Work on Man's Conscience

Revelation 12:10 says, "The accuser of our brothers...who accuses them before our God day and night." This shows us that part of Satan's work is to accuse us. This work is carried out in man's conscience. As soon as a person is saved, his conscience is quickened, and he begins to know sin. Satan knows this. He knows that the Holy Spirit touches the conscience of God's children concerning sin. He knows that He guides them into confession and prayer for forgiveness before God. Consequently, Satan steps in to counterfeit the Holy Spirit's work. He accuses man in his conscience. Such an attack is found frequently among God's children, and it causes much havoc.

Many children of God cannot differentiate between the Holy Spirit's reproach and Satan's accusation. As a result, they are hesitant to withstand anything. This gives Satan further ground to exercise his accusations. Many children of God could have been very useful in the hands of God, but their conscience has been weakened to the uttermost by Satan's attack. They are bombarded constantly with the accusation and feeling that they have sinned in this and that matter. They are unable to stand up before God or before men. As a result, they become spiritually handicapped for the rest of their lives.

It is true that we should pay attention to the reproach of the Holy Spirit once we become Christians. However, we also need to withstand Satan's accusation. We need to pay attention to the difference between the Holy Spirit's reproach and Satan's accusation. Many so-called reproaches are counterfeits; they are, in fact, Satan's accusations.

1. The Difference between Satan's Accusation and the Holy Spirit's Reproach

What is the difference between Satan's accusation and the Holy Spirit's reproach? We need to distinguish between them.

First, all reproaches from the Holy Spirit begin with a small feeling from within. This inner feeling becomes stronger and stronger and convicts us of our mistakes. Satan's accusation, however, is a continual nagging within. The reproach of the Holy Spirit grows stronger and stronger as time goes on; the accusation of Satan is the same from beginning to end. As time passes, the inner sense of the Spirit ascends by degree; but the accusation of Satan is a constant, muddled nagging that stays the same from beginning to end.

Second, each time we yield to the rebuke of the Spirit, we find the power of sin diminishing in us. Each rebuke of the Spirit diminishes the power of sin a little. Therefore, any rebuke from the Spirit weakens the power of sin; it results in a diminishing of sin. This is not the case with Satan's accusation. Every time he accuses us, we find the power of sin to be just as great as before.

Third, the reproach of the Holy Spirit brings us to the Lord, whereas Satan's accusation brings us disappointment. The more we are reproved by the Holy Spirit, the more we are strengthened within to deal with our problem before the Lord. But Satan's accusation brings about despair and resignation. The reproach of the Holy Spirit causes us to come before the Lord and to rely on Him; Satan's accusation causes us to turn back to ourselves and to be disappointed.

Fourth, if it is the reproach of the Holy Spirit, confession before the Lord will follow. This confession will result in at least peace, if not joy. There may or may not be joy, but there is always peace. Satan's accusation, however, is totally different. There is no joy and no peace, even after one confesses his sins. This is like coming out of a major illness or going through a theatrical performance—nothing remains after the act is over. The reproach of the Holy Spirit has a result—peace, if not joy. However, Satan's accusation leads us nowhere.

Fifth, the reproach of the Holy Spirit reminds us of the blood of the Lord. With Satan's accusation, there is always the Satan-injected thought: "There is not much use. Perhaps the Lord will not forgive you." This thought will be there even when we know that we have the blood. In other words, the reproach of the Holy Spirit leads to faith in the Lord's blood, while Satan's accusation causes us to lose our faith in the Lord's blood. When a certain feeling comes, simply check whether we are reminded of the blood as a result of this feeling or whether we have been distanced from the blood. This will tell us whether the feeling is a reproach of the Holy Spirit or an accusation from Satan.

Sixth, the result of the reproach of the Holy Spirit is power from God; one will rise up on his feet and run faster. He will go on with renewed zeal, cast aside his trust in himself, and have more faith in God. However, the result of Satan's accusation is the debilitation of the conscience. The conscience of such ones is smitten before God. They have no faith in themselves, and they have no faith in God either. It is true that the reproach of the Holy Spirit takes away our strength and our trust in ourselves. But at the same time it causes us to have more faith in the Lord. Satan's accusation is not like this. It takes away our confidence in ourselves as well as our faith in the Lord. The result is that we become a debilitated person.

2. How to Overcome Satan's Accusation

Revelation 12:11 says, "And they (the brothers) overcame him because of the blood of the Lamb and because of the word of their testimony, and they loved not their soul-life even unto death." *Him* here refers to Satan, who accused the brothers. How do we overcome him?

First, we overcome by the blood of the Lamb. On the one hand, when we sin before the Lord, we must confess our sins. On the other hand, we must say to Satan, "There is no need for you to accuse me! I come before the Lord today by the blood of the Lord!" To overcome Satan, we must show him that we are forgiven through the blood of the Lamb. All our sins, major or minor, have been forgiven through the blood of the Lamb. This is the Word of God: "The blood of Jesus His Son cleanses us from every sin" (1 John 1:7). We must realize that the blood of the Lamb is the basis of our forgiveness before God as well as the basis of our acceptance in Him. We should not be so presumptuous as to think that we are good. Neither should we be so foolish as to condemn ourselves from morning to evening. It is foolish to be proud, and it is also foolish to keep looking at oneself. Those who consider themselves to be good are foolish, and those who are blind to the saving power of the Lord are foolish as well. Those who believe in their own power are foolish, and those who do not believe in the Lord's power are foolish as well. We must see that the blood of the Lamb has already fulfilled all the demands of God. It has also overcome all the accusations of Satan.

Second, we overcome because of the word of our testimony. This word of our testimony declares the spiritual facts; it declares the victory of the Lord. We must tell Satan, "There is no need for you to trouble me! My sins have been forgiven through the Lord's blood!" We need to exercise our faith to declare that Jesus is Lord and that He has won the victory. We need to speak out the word of our testimony and let Satan hear this word. We must not only believe in our hearts but also declare it to Satan with our mouth. This is the word of our testimony.

Third, we must not love our soul-life even unto death. "The blood of the Lamb" and "the word of their testimony" spoken of previously are two conditions for victory over Satan. The refusal to love one's soul-life even unto death is an attitude. No matter what Satan is doing, even if he is putting us to death, our attitude should be such that we still trust in the blood of the Lamb and still declare His victory. Satan's accusation will stop if we stand fast in this way. He cannot overcome us. Instead, we will surely overcome him!

Some brothers and sisters receive so much accusation from Satan that they can no longer discern whether it is an accusation from Satan or a reproach of the Holy Spirit. They should stop confessing their sins for a while; the Lord does not want us to do things foolishly. Instead, they should pray to the Lord and say, "If I have sinned, I will confess my sins and ask for Your forgiveness. But now I am under Satan's accusation. I pray that You cover all my sins. From this point on, everything is under Your blood, and I will not be bothered by anything anymore, whether it be sin or otherwise!" Those who are in such a condition must forget about everything for a while before they can differentiate clearly between Satan's accusation and the Holy Spirit's reproach.

3. How to Help Those Who Are under Satan's Accusation

We must never add to the burden of the conscience of those under Satan's accusation. First, we should help them to do only what is within their ability to handle. If we ask them to do what is beyond their ability, they will fall easily into condemnation. We must be sure that they have enough strength before the Lord to go on before we give them stronger advice or urge them to move ahead. Second, where there is the clear work of the Holy Spirit, we should raise the standard a little, for with the clear operation of the Spirit of the Lord and the spirit of revival, the Lord's word has the ability to uplift the capacity of a person. If we raise the standard very high when the Spirit of the Lord has not done anything, we are not helping these accused ones to go on; rather, we are giving Satan opportunities to accuse them even more.

We must not be careless in pointing out the failures of others. Suppose a brother has failed in certain areas, yet he can still pray, read the Bible, and attend the meetings. As long as you have the assurance within that you can help him, a little push may be all that is necessary to bring him through his trouble. But if you do not have the assurance within and you do not have the power to uplift him, your exposure of his failures will only quench his prayers, his reading of the Bible, and his meeting life. The smoking flax must be rekindled; it must not be smothered. The bruised reed must be supported; it must not be broken. We should not make ourselves the standard and put the conscience of others under condemnation. We must learn not to do things that would offend the conscience of others.

We must point out Hebrews 10:22 to those who are under Satan's accusation: "Having our hearts sprinkled from an evil conscience." With such a sprinkling, our conscience should no longer feel guilty. The principle of the Christian life is a life free from any condemnation in the conscience. When a Christian is condemned in his conscience, he will be weak before God and will be debilitated in all spiritual matters. Satan's goal is to derail us from this principle. This is the reason he accuses us unceasingly. We need to lay hold of this principle by applying the blood. The more Satan tries to make us feel guilty, the more we should apply the blood to all of our sins. The brothers overcame him not by their own strength, but by the blood of the Lamb. We can declare, "Satan, I admit that I have sinned. But I have been redeemed by the Lord! I have never denied that I am a debtor. I am in debt, but the Lord has paid my debt!" We do not need to deal with Satan's accusation by denying that we are debtors. We can deal with him by declaring that our debt has been paid.

D. Satan's Work in the Environment

All circumstances are arranged by God. However, there are many things in our environment which, though permitted by God, are the result of Satan's direct and active work.

Take Job's experience as an example. His oxen and donkeys were taken away, his house collapsed, and his children were killed. These were all things in the environment. Though they were permitted by God, Satan was the one directly instigating the attacks.

Peter's failure was another example. The cause of his fall was partly due to himself, but partly due to Satan's attack in the environment. The Lord said, "Simon, Simon, behold, Satan has asked to have you all to sift you as wheat" (Luke 22:31). Peter's fall was the direct result of Satan's work. Yet it was something permitted by God.

Paul's thorn was clearly the work of Satan. Paul said, "There was given to me a thorn in the flesh, a messenger of

Satan, that he might buffet me" (2 Cor. 12:7). This is the work of Satan. It is Satan who attacks God's children in the environment.

An even clearer example can be seen in Matthew 8, when the Lord Jesus ordered the disciples to depart to the other side of the sea. He knew that powerful demons had to be cast out on the other side of the sea. After He and the disciples stepped into the boat, suddenly a great tempest arose in the sea so that the boat was covered by the waves. The Lord was asleep. The disciples came near and roused Him, saying, "Lord, save us; we are perishing!" (v. 25). A few of the disciples were fishermen; they were very experienced sailors. However, they realized that the waves were more than they could handle. The Lord Jesus rebuked their little faith; then He rose and rebuked the winds and the sea. The winds and the sea have no personality of their own, yet the Lord rebuked them because the devil was behind them. Satan had stirred up the winds and the waves.

In conclusion, Satan not only attacks our body, our conscience, and our mind, but also attacks us through our environment.

How should we react to Satan's attack in the environment?

First, we must humble ourselves under the mighty hand of God. Both James 4 and 1 Peter 5 tell us to withstand Satan. These two portions also tell us to humble ourselves before God. When Satan attacks us in the environment, our first reaction should be to submit to God. We cannot withstand the devil if we do not submit to God. Our conscience will condemn us if we withstand the devil without submitting to God. Therefore, our first reaction should be to submit to God.

Second, we should withstand the devil. When God's children encounter unreasonable and inexplicable things in the environment and have the clear sense within that these are attacks from Satan, they should withstand him. Once they withstand, the attacks will be behind them. On the one hand, they need to humble themselves under the hand of God. On the other hand, they must withstand Satan's work in the environment. When they humble themselves, and their attitude before God is firm, God will show them that it is not Him but Satan who is doing the work. Thus, they will be able to differentiate God's arrangement from Satan's attack. Once they are clear and once they withstand the devil, the attacks will go away.

Third, we must reject all forms of fear. Satan has to find a lodging ground before he can work on God's children. He cannot work where he has no ground to work. Therefore, his first attack is to gain a beachhead. He then attacks us from this beachhead. We should not give any ground to him. This is the way to victory. There is one area which can become Satan's greatest stronghold—fear. When Satan tries to put us through trials, the first thing he does is to put fear into us. An experienced sister once said, "Fear is Satan's calling card." Once you accept fear, Satan steps in. If you reject fear, he will not be able to come in.

All thoughts of fear are attacks from Satan. Whatever you are afraid of, you will surely experience. Job said, "For I dread something, and it comes upon me; / And what I fear comes to me" (Job 3:25). Job experienced everything that he feared. Satan's attack in the environment comes mostly in the form of fear. If you withstand the fear, the things that you fear will not come. But if you allow the fear to remain, you will give Satan the opportunity to do the very things that you fear.

Therefore, in order for God's children to withstand the work of Satan, the first thing they have to reject is fear. When Satan puts a fear in you for this or that thing, you must not give in to this fear. You should say, "I will never accept what the Lord has not measured to me!" Once a person is delivered from fear, he is delivered from Satan's realm. This is what Paul meant when he said, "Neither give place to the devil" (Eph. 4:27).

Why do we not need to fear? We do not fear "because greater is He who is in you than he who is in the world" (1 John 4:4). If we are fearful, it is because we are ignorant of this fact.

II. WITHSTANDING SATAN BY FAITH

First Peter 5:8-9 says, "Be sober; watch. Your adversary, the devil, as a roaring lion, walks about, seeking someone to devour. Him withstand, being firm in your faith." God's Word shows us clearly that the way to withstand Satan is by faith. There is no other way to withstand him. What should our faith rest on? How should we exercise our faith to withstand him? Let us consider what the Word of God says concerning this.

A. Believing That the Lord's Manifestation Is to Destroy the Works of the Devil

First, we must believe that the Lord was manifested for the purpose of destroying the works of the devil (1 John 3:8). The Son of God has come to the earth; He was manifested. When He was on earth, He destroyed the work of the devil wherever He went. Often Satan's work was not obvious; he hid behind natural phenomena. However, the Lord rebuked him every time. It is clear that He was rebuking Satan when He rebuked Peter's speaking (Matt. 16:22-23), when He rebuked the fever of Peter's mother-in-law (Luke 4:39), and when He rebuked the winds and the waves. Although the devil hid behind many natural phenomena, the Lord Jesus rebuked him. Wherever the Lord went, the power of the devil was shattered. This is why He said, "But if I, by the Spirit of God, cast out the demons, then the kingdom of God has come upon you" (Matt. 12:28). In other words, wherever the Lord went, Satan was cast out, and the kingdom of God was manifested. Satan could not remain where the Lord was. This is why He said that He was manifested to destroy the works of the devil.

We should also believe that in manifesting Himself on the earth, the Lord not only destroyed the works of the devil, but also gave authority to His disciples to cast out demons in His name. The Lord said, "Behold, I have given you the authority to tread upon serpents and scorpions and over all the power of the enemy" (Luke 10:19). He gave His name to the church so that His church might continue His work on earth after His ascension. The Lord used His authority on earth to cast out demons. He also gave this authority to the church.

We must distinguish between what the devil has and what we have. What the devil has is power. What we have is authority. All that Satan has is power. But the Lord Jesus has given us authority, which can overcome all the power of Satan. Power cannot prevail over authority. God has given us authority, and Satan will surely fail.

Consider an illustration of how authority overcomes power: A traffic light on a road controls traffic. When a policeman turns on the red light, all pedestrians and cars have to stop. No one is allowed to dash through a red light. The pedestrians and cars are much more powerful than the red light in terms of power. However, no pedestrian or driver will dare dash through the red light because of the presence of authority. This is an example of authority prevailing over power.

Authority prevails over power; this is God's established policy in this universe. No matter how strong Satan's power is, one fact remains sure—the Lord Jesus has given His name to the church. This name stands for authority. The church can cast out demons in the name of the Lord. We can invoke the Lord's name to deal with Satan's power. Thank God that no matter how great Satan's power is, the Lord's name is immeasurably greater. The authority behind the Lord's name is strong enough to overcome all the power of Satan.

The disciples went out in the name of the Lord. They were surprised when they returned. They told the Lord, "Lord, even the demons are subject to us in Your name" (10:17). The Lord's name spells authority. His giving of His name to us means that He has given His authority to us. The Lord said, "Behold, I have given you the authority to tread upon serpents and scorpions and over all the power of the enemy, and nothing shall by any means hurt you" (v. 19). Whoever desires to withstand Satan must learn to know the difference between the Lord's authority and Satan's power. No matter how great Satan's power is, the Lord's authority is able to overcome him. We must believe that God has given this authority to the church. The church can cast out demons and withstand the devil in the name of the Lord Jesus.

B. Believing That the Lord's Death Has Destroyed Satan

Second, we must believe that through death the Lord Jesus has destroyed him who has the might of death, the devil (Heb.

2:14). The manifestation of the Lord Jesus destroyed the works of the devil, and the death of the Lord Jesus destroyed the devil himself.

The Lord's death pronounces the greatest defeat for the devil because the Lord's death is not only a punishment but also a way of salvation. In Genesis 2:17 God spoke of death: "For in the day that thou eatest thereof thou shalt surely die." This death is surely a punishment. Satan was delighted at this word. Since man would die if he ate the fruit, Satan tried his best to seduce man to eat it, so that death would reign in man and he could claim the victory. However, the Lord's death constitutes the greatest way of salvation. It is true that God said, "For in the day that thou eatest thereof thou shalt surely die." This death is punishment. But the Lord has another death. The second death is a way of salvation. Death can punish those who sin. Death can also save and deliver those who are in sin. Satan thought that death could only punish the sinner. He seized upon this fact and reigned through man's death. However, God saves and delivers man from sin through the death of the Lord Jesus. This is the most profound aspect of the gospel.

The Lord's death on the cross takes away not only our sins but also the whole old creation. Our old man has been crucified with him. Although Satan reigns through death, the more he reigns through death, the worse his lot becomes, because his reign stops at death. Since we are already dead, death can no longer sting us. He has no further reign over us.

"For in the day that thou eatest thereof thou shalt surely die." God said this so that man would not eat of the fruit of the tree of the knowledge of good and evil. But man ate it and sinned. What then should be done? The result of sin is death; there is no way to change this. However, there is a way to salvation, a salvation which goes through death. When the Lord Jesus was crucified on the cross for us, the old creation and the old man were both crucified with Him. This means that Satan's authority can only go as far as death. The Scripture says, "Through death He might destroy him who has the might of death, that is, the devil" (Heb. 2:14).

Thank and praise the Lord. We are those who are already

dead. If Satan attacks us, we can say to him, "I am already dead!" He has no authority over us because we are already dead. His authority extends only to the point of death.

Our crucifixion with Christ is an accomplished fact; it is God's doing. The Bible does not say that our death with the Lord is something that belongs to the future. It is not some experience that we hope to attain one day. The Bible does not tell us to pursue death. It shows us that we are already dead. A person is not dead if he is still pursuing death. However, our death with Christ is a gift from God in the same way that His death for us is a gift. If a man is still pursuing crucifixion, he is standing on fleshly ground, and Satan has full control over those who stand on fleshly ground. We must believe in the Lord's death. We must also believe in our own death. Just as we believed in the Lord's death for us, so also we should believe in our death in Him. Both are acts of faith, and neither has anything to do with human pursuits. As soon as we strive to realize these facts, we expose ourselves to Satan's attack. We have to lay hold of the accomplished facts and declare: "Praise and thank the Lord; I am already dead."

We must see that, in the eyes of God, our death with Christ is an accomplished fact. Once we see this, Satan can no longer do anything with us. Satan can deal only with those who are not dead. He can rule over only those who are facing death and who are on their way to death. But we are no longer facing death; we have already died. Satan can do nothing about us.

In order to withstand Satan, we must realize that the Lord's manifestation was a manifestation of authority, and the work of His cross has released all those who are under Satan's hand. Satan no longer has any authority over us anymore. We are above him. We are those who are already dead. Satan's way is terminated by death, and there is nothing more that he can do.

C. Believing That the Lord's Resurrection Has Put Satan to Shame

Third, we must believe that the Lord's resurrection has put Satan to shame. Satan no longer has any way to attack us.

Colossians 2:12 says, "Buried together with Him in baptism, in which also you were raised together with Him through the faith of the operation of God, who raised Him from the dead." This verse speaks of death as well as resurrection. Verse 13 tells us how we died and resurrected; verse 14 tells us what the Lord did at the time of His death; and verse 15 says that the Lord Jesus stripped off the rulers and the authorities and "made a display of them openly, triumphing over them in it." Verse 20 says, "If you died with Christ," and 3:1 says, "If therefore you were raised together with Christ." These verses begin with resurrection and end with resurrection, and the verses in between speak of triumphing in the cross. We stand in the position of resurrection, and we triumph in the cross.

Why can we do this? The statement we made earlier explains this: The Lord has died, and we also are dead in Him. Satan, who has dominion over the old man, can follow us only as far as the cross. Resurrection is beyond him. Just as Satan had nothing in the Lord Jesus while He was on earth (John 14:30), so also he has nothing in Him in resurrection. Satan has no place at all in the new life. He has no authority at all in the new life and cannot touch our new life!

When the Lord was hung on the cross, it seemed as if myriads of demons were surrounding it. They thought that they could destroy the Son of God. It was to have been their greatest victory. Little did they realize that the Lord Jesus would go into death, come out of death, and overcome the authority of death! Here is the glorious fact: The Lord has come out of death! Therefore, we have the boldness and the confidence to say that the life of God is well able to cast away death!

What is the resurrection life? The resurrection life is a life that cannot be touched by death. It is a life that transcends death, that is beyond the boundary of death, that comes out of death, and that death cannot hold. Satan's power extends only as far as death. The Lord Jesus proved how great the power of His life is through His resurrection. He dismantled the power of Satan. The Bible calls this power "the power of His resurrection" (Phil. 3:10). When this resurrection power is expressed through us, everything of Satan is cast down!

We can withstand Satan because our life is a life of resurrection. This life has nothing to do with Satan. Our life issues from the life of God; it is a life that comes out of death. Satan's power only goes as far as death. Whatever it does to us is limited to this side of death. But our life has come out of death. We have a life which he cannot touch. We are standing on resurrection ground, and we look back in triumph through the cross. Colossians 2 speaks of triumphing in resurrection. It is a chapter on resurrection, not death. We do not triumph in death through resurrection; rather we triumph in resurrection through death.

In order to withstand Satan, every child of God must declare with a strong faith, "Thank God, I have resurrected! Satan, what can you do? What you can do goes only so far as death. But the life that I have today has nothing to do with you! This life has been tested by you already. What else can you do? You are powerless! This life has transcended over you! Satan, get away from me!"

We cannot deal with Satan on the ground of hope. We can only stand on the ground of resurrection, the ground of the Lord. This is a very basic principle. Colossians 2:12 tells us that we must believe in "the operation of God, who raised Him from the dead."

We need to take the same position before Satan as that which we take before God. The Bible tells us to put on the robe of righteousness when we come before God (Isa. 61:10; Zech. 3:4-5). Our robe of righteousness is Christ. We need to put on Christ to come before God. In the same way, we need to put on Christ to come before Satan. God cannot find our sins when we put on Christ. Likewise, Satan cannot find our sins when we are in Christ. When we take this stand, Satan can no longer attack us. We are perfect before God and perfect also before Satan. What a glorious fact!

We must not be afraid of Satan. If we are afraid of Satan, he will laugh at us. He will say, "What a fool there is on earth. How can this one be so foolish?" Anyone who is afraid of Satan is foolish, because he has forgotten his position in Christ. We have no reason to fear him. We have transcended over his power. We can stand before him and say, "You cannot touch me! No matter how strong and resourceful you are, you are still one step behind!" On the day of the Lord's resurrection, He led the enemy captive and openly shamed him. Today we are standing on the ground of resurrection, and we triumph through the cross!

D. Believing That the Ascension of the Lord Is Far above the Power of Satan

Fourth, we must believe that the ascension of the Lord has put Him far above the power of Satan. Ephesians 1:20-22 says, "Raising Him from the dead and seating Him at His right hand in the heavenlies, far above all...not only in this age but also in that which is to come; and He subjected all things under His feet and gave Him to be Head over all things to the church." This means that the Lord Jesus is already seated in the heavenlies and is far above all the power of Satan.

Ephesians 2:6 says, "And raised us up together with Him and seated us together with Him in the heavenlies in Christ Jesus." This is our position, the position of a Christian. The Lord Jesus is resurrected; He is seated in the heavenlies far above all the power of Satan. We are raised up together with Christ and are seated together with Him in the heavenlies, far above all the power of Satan.

Ephesians 6:11 and 13 say, "Put on the whole armor of God that you may be able to stand against the stratagems of the devil....and having done all, to stand." Chapter two shows us that we are seated together with the Lord in the heavenlies. Chapter six shows us that we need to stand firm. Chapter two says that we need to sit, while chapter six says that we need to stand. What does it mean to sit? To sit means to rest. It means that the Lord has overcome and that we can now rest in His victory. This is what it means to depend on the Lord's victory. What does it mean to stand? To stand means that spiritual warfare is not a matter of assault but of defense. To stand does not mean to attack; it means to defend. Because the Lord has overcome completely, we have no need to attack again. The victory of the cross is complete, and there is no further need to attack. Here we see two attitudes: One is to sit, and the other is to stand. To sit is to rest in the Lord's victory, while to stand is to withstand Satan and to stop him from taking away our victory.

Christian warfare is a matter of warding off defeat; it is not a matter of fighting for victory. We have already overcome. We fight from the position of victory, and we fight to maintain our victory. We are not fighting to win a victory. We fight from victory; victory is something that is in our hands. The warfare spoken of in Ephesians is the warfare of the overcomers. We do not become overcomers through fighting. We need to distinguish between these two things.

How does Satan tempt us? He causes us to forget our own position and our victory. He blinds our eyes to our own victory. If we give in to his tactics, we will feel that victory is far away and beyond our reach. We must remember that the victory of the Lord is complete. It is so complete that our whole life is included in this victory! Once we believe, we overcome. Satan is defeated and we have overcome in Christ. Satan wants to steal away the victory which we have gained. His work is to taunt us to secretly find out if we still have the faith. If we do not know that victory is already ours, we will fail. But if we know our victory, his work will fail.

Therefore, we counter the work of Satan with the work of the Lord Jesus. We withstand Satan through the Lord's manifestation, death, resurrection, and ascension. We are standing today upon the accomplished work of the Lord. We do not need to *try* to overcome in any way when Satan attacks us. Once we have the slightest thought of trying to overcome, we have failed, because our position is wrong. How great is the difference between a person who tries to overcome and one who withstands by knowing that he has already overcome. To withstand the devil means that we withstand him by the victory of Christ.

This matter indeed needs revelation. We need to see the manifestation of the Lord. We need to see His death, resurrection, and ascension. We need to know all these things.

As Christians we must learn to withstand the devil. We must say to Satan under all circumstances, "Get away from me!" May God be gracious to us so that we may all have such a faith. May we have faith toward the four things the Lord has accomplished for us, and may we exercise strong faith to withstand Satan and reject his work upon us.